GRAY BLACK

Colors can make you
feel different each day,
so what will you paint in
your picture today?

PURPLE

sunny   happy   joyful   smiley

yellow

Paint me some SUNSHINE to make the flowers grow.

Paint me

some

Red

balloons

tied up with a bow.

PASSIONATE

BOLd

dANGErOUS

COURAGEOUS

BRAVE

Paint me the **BLUE** SEA to sail on FAR AND wide.

floating

calm wise peaceful

relaxed

energetic

FUN thoughtful lo

Paint me a

PiNK dress

to twirl in with pride.

pure
bright reflective light

Paint me some

WHite

STARS

to help light

my way!

clEAR

Paint me

some

ORANge

leaves

to tumble in and play.

Paint me some **GReeN** Hills for our favorite place.

gentle

HEALTHY NATURAL HARMONIOUS

Paint me a PURPLE

BIKE ON WHICH
I CAN RACE.

AMBITIOUS

INDEPENDENT CREATIVE
magical

Here are the **PRIMARY COLORS** for you,
they only exist as red, yellow and blue.

The **SECONDARY COLORS**
are made from these three...

+

...mix them together and what
do you see?

+

+

WHAT OTHER COLORS
CAN YOU MAKE?

Yellow Blue
Red Black
Pink Green